HENRY AND MUDGE
AND THE
FUNNY LUNCH

The Twenty-Fourth Book of Their Adventures

by Cynthia Rylant
illustrated by Carolyn Bracken
in the style of Suçie Stevenson

READY-TO-READ

SIMON & SCHUSTER BOOKS FOR YOUNG READERS
New York   London   Toronto   Sydney   Singapore

THE HENRY AND MUDGE BOOKS

SIMON & SCHUSTER BOOKS FOR YOUNG READERS
An imprint of Simon & Schuster Children's Publishing Division
1230 Avenue of the Americas
New York, New York 10020
Text copyright © 2004 by Cynthia Rylant
Illustrations copyright © 2004 by Suçie Stevenson
SIMON & SCHUSTER BOOKS FOR YOUNG READERS is a trademark of Simon & Schuster, Inc.
READY-TO-READ is a registered trademark of Simon & Schuster, Inc.
Book design by Mark Siegel
The text for this book is set in 18-point Goudy.
The illustrations are rendered in pen-and-ink and watercolor.
Manufactured in the United States of America
10 9 8 7 6 5 4 3 2 1
CIP data for this book is available from the Library of Congress.
ISBN 0-689-81178-0

Contents

Mother's Day

One day in May, Henry and Henry's
big dog, Mudge, were playing kickball
with some friends.

(Kickball was better than catch
because no one had to pick up the
drooly ball.)

5

Suddenly Henry remembered something:
Mother's Day!

Henry and his dad always made a funny
lunch for Henry's mother on Mother's Day.

One year they made a Tomato Snowman.

Another year they baked a
Sweet Potato Shoe.

Mother's Day was only a day away.
What would they make for lunch this year?

"Let's go find Dad, Mudge," Henry
said, heading home.
Mudge shook hands with all of
Henry's friends before leaving.
Mudge had very good manners.

Henry's father hadn't forgotten
Mother's Day.

When Henry got home, his dad was
making a grocery list.
"What are we fixing for Mother's Day
lunch?" Henry asked.

Henry's father smiled.

"Something juicy," he said.

Mudge wagged.

He liked juicy things.

12

"Something crunchy," said
Henry's father.
Mudge wagged again.
He liked crunchy things, too.

"Something you can really stretch out on!" Henry's father said.
"Something juicy and crunchy that you can stretch out on?" asked Henry.
"What in the world is it?"

"A Pineapple Sofa!"
said Henry's father.

Mudge wagged and wagged and wagged. "Juicy" and "Crunchy" and "Sofa" were some of his favorite words!

Shopping

Henry and Mudge went grocery
shopping with Henry's father.
The grocery store owner was a
cousin of Henry's father, so he
always let Mudge in.

Mudge *loved* grocery shopping.

He got crackers as soon as he came through the door. While Henry and Henry's father bought things for a Pineapple Sofa, Mudge walked around and sniffed.

He sniffed and sniffed and sniffed.

He sniffed the Fruity Puffs.

He sniffed the Cocoa Chews.

He even sniffed the Fishy Flakes.

23

No one minded because everyone in the
store loved Mudge.

24

Babies gave him their suckers and grandmas
rubbed his head.
They were all glad to see him.

Soon the shopping was done.
Henry and Mudge and Henry's father
headed home.
Henry and his dad laughed about the
Pineapple Sofa they were going to make.

27

Henry's dad said that maybe it should
be a sleep sofa.
He said that maybe it should pull out
into a Watermelon Bed.
Henry giggled and giggled.
He loved making funny food.

29

Yum!

On Mother's Day Henry and
Henry's father got to work.
They cut pineapple cushions.
They fixed marshmallow pillows.

31

They made an apple father,

a peach mother,

a plum boy,

and a kiwi dog.

Then they set everything on top of a
giant chocolate bar and served it to
Henry's mother.

"Happy Mother's Day!" said Henry.

"Yum!" said Henry's mother, clapping
her hands.

She shared the Pineapple Sofa with everyone,
then gave each of them a big kiss.

Later, as they rested on their *real* sofa, Henry's father said to Henry, "What if next year we do a French Fry Cat?"

Mudge wagged and wagged
and wagged.